A Flower in the Snow

For Anna, who has always loved Bear...
All my love, TC xx

For the bears in my family—SA

First published in Great Britain in 2012 by Egmont UK Limited

ISBN 978-0-545-61151-0

12 11 10 9 8 7 6 5 4 3 2 1   14 15 16 17 18 19/0

Printed in the U.S.A.   08

This edition first printing, September 2014

Cover design by Rose Audette

A Flower in the Snow

Tracey Corderoy   Sophie Allsopp

SCHOLASTIC INC.

In an icy kingdom far away, lived a little girl called Luna.

Her happy smile sparkled
like the snow.

Luna loved to dance through
the snowflakes or catch them
on her tongue...

...or leave little tiptoe patterns everywhere!

But there was one thing Luna loved more than all of these. He was big and soft and cuddly and was Luna's best friend...

Bear.

Luna and Bear belonged together, like peanut butter and jelly!

And everything they did, they did together...

Skating on the frozen lake...

...rolling giant snowballs,

or even
catching
a cold!

Luna lived in an igloo...

...and Bear lived in a snow cave in her little garden
where, one bright day, something most unusual popped
up. It was a flower—a dancing yellow flower!

How pretty it is, thought Bear.

Then, carefully, he picked it for someone special...

"Just look at its face!" smiled Luna.
"My little sunshine flower!
I've never seen anything so
beautiful—I'll treasure it
forever!"

But, all too soon, her flower
wilted, and as the last petal
fell, so Luna's sparkly smile
disappeared...

and nothing...

would bring it back.

Eventually Bear knew what he had to do to bring back
Luna's smile. So away he sailed to find another sunshine flower...

The next day Luna searched everywhere for Bear. Then, at last, she found a note...

Gone to find a sunshine flower.
Bear x x

From then on, every night, Luna would gaze at the moon.
"Please come home tomorrow, Bear," she'd whisper.

And, every morning, she'd rush to his
cave and peep through the little window.

"Bear!" she'd call...

...but he was never there.

Far, far away, Bear searched for his special gift for Luna.

Along dusty,
windswept tracks...

on through deep, dark jungles...

...down soft, grassy
hillsides...

and across hot, sandy deserts.
But, though he hunted high and low...

...he couldn't find a sunshine flower.

Then, one crisp and twinkly night,
a snowflake kissed his nose.

How good it felt—so cold and light!
It was time to go home to Luna.

So Bear set sail once again and tall
waves tossed his boat.

Through days and nights
he held on tight...

...until, at last, he landed
on the icy shores of home.

Bear was sad that he had no gift for Luna,
but seeing her again was all that mattered.

But Luna wasn't dancing through
the snowflakes or making tiptoe
patterns in the snow like she used to.

Bear began to worry...

and then...

...he saw her!

"Bear!" cried Luna. "You came home!"

"But I didn't bring your gift," Bear answered sadly.
"Oh, Bear," smiled Luna. "You are my gift!
As long as you are here with me, I'm happy."

Then, taking his big,
soft paw, "Bear, come
with me," she said.
"There's something
very special I have
to show you..."

"When the last petal fell from the sunshine
flower, some little seeds were left.
So I planted one," smiled Luna,
"and watered it every day!
And look what grew..."

"...*another* sunshine flower!"

Then, from her pocket, she took Bear's note and carefully unwrapped it...

"I've been saving these seeds to plant with you," she said.

So Luna and Bear planted the seeds and cared for them each day. And, before long...

...a sunshine meadow

Now hiding among the flowers are butterflies and bees...

danced in the snow!

...and snails and spotted ladybugs...

...and two very best friends.